MEL BAY'S EASIEST FINGERPICKING GUITAR BOOK

By William Bay & Tommy Flint

2 3 4 5 6 7 8 9 0

The six open strings of the guitar are of the same pitch as the six notes shown in the illustration of the piano keyboard. Note that five of the strings are below the middle C of the piano keyboard.

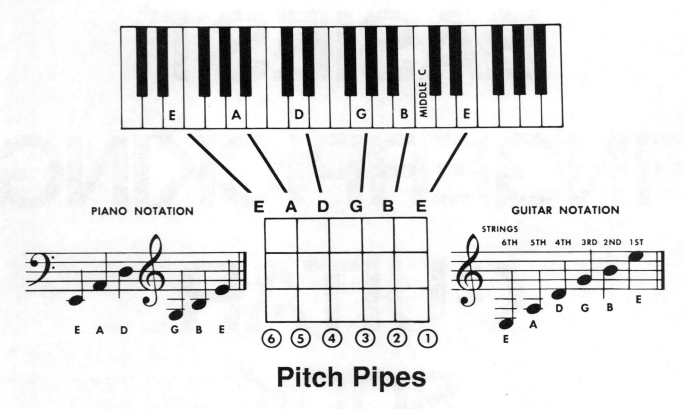

Pitch Pipes

Pitch pipes with instructions for their use may be obtained at any music store.
Pitch pipes have the correct pitch of each guitar string and are recommended to be used when a piano is not available.

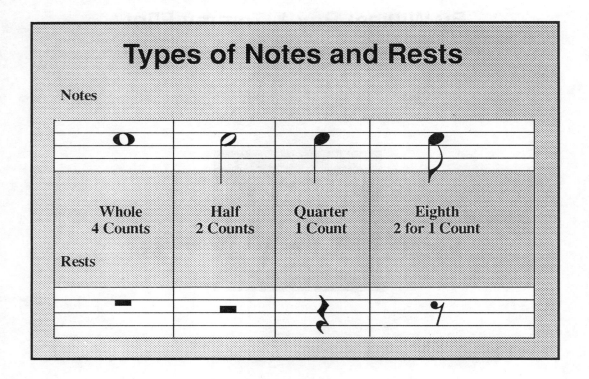

Types of Notes and Rests

Notes			
Whole 4 Counts	Half 2 Counts	Quarter 1 Count	Eighth 2 for 1 Count
Rests			

EXPLANATION OF CHORD SYMBOLS

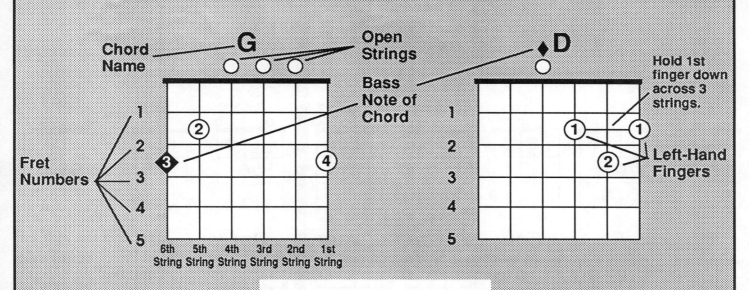

Chord Name
Open Strings
Bass Note of Chord
Fret Numbers
Hold 1st finger down across 3 strings.
Left-Hand Fingers

G   D

6th String 5th String 4th String 3rd String 2nd String 1st String

Time Signatures

C or **4/4** (4 beats per measure.) (A quarter note receives one beat.)

Count: 1-2-3-4, 1-2-3-4, etc.

2/4 (2 beats per measure.) (A quarter note receives one beat.)

Count: 1-2, 1-2, etc.

3/4 (3 beats per measure.) (A quarter note receives one beat.)

Count: 1-2-3, 1-2-3, etc.

6/8 (6 beats per measure.) (An eighth note receives one beat.)

Count: **1**-2-3-**4**-5-6, **1**-2-3-**4**-5-6, etc.
(Accent beats 1 and 4.)

Right-Hand Positioning

P = Pulgar = Thumb
I = Indicio = Index Finger
M = Medio = Middle Finger
A = Anular = Ring Finger

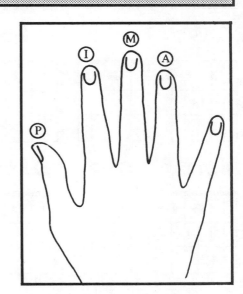

3

Major Key · Relative Minor

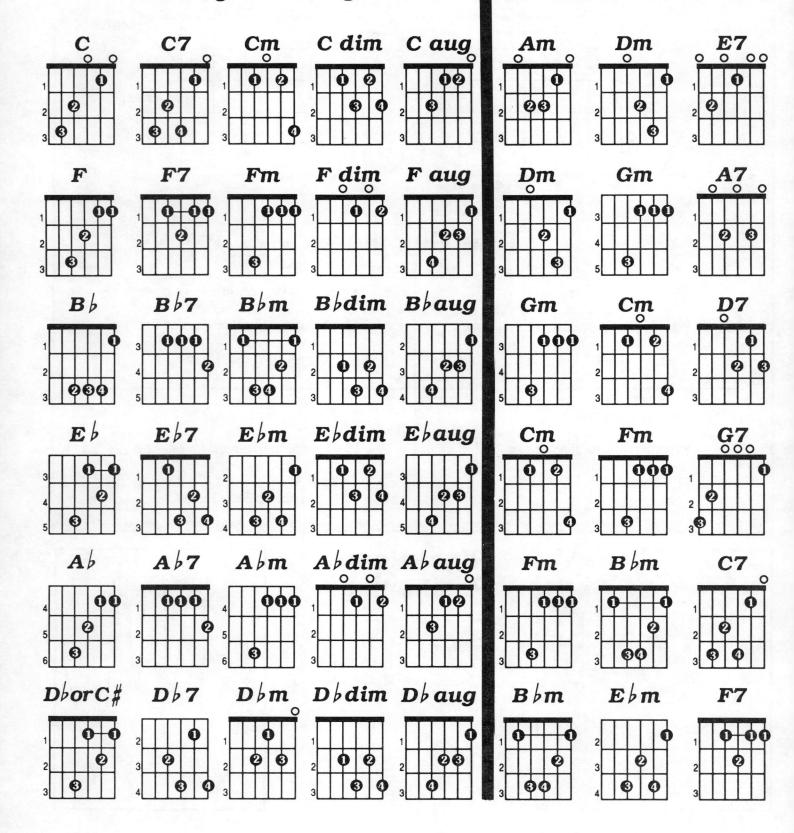

Major Key　Relative Minor

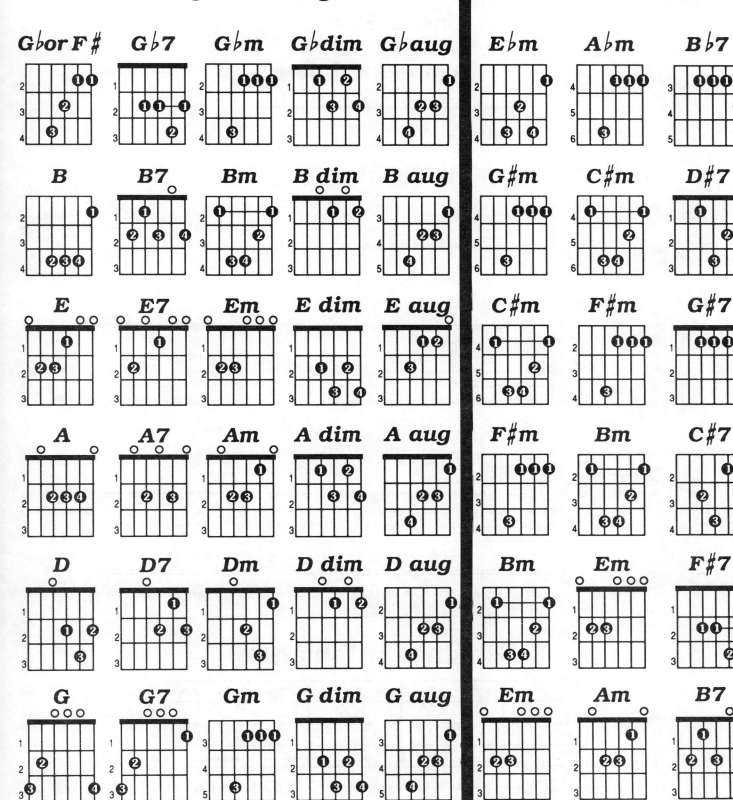

Tablature is a way of writing guitar music which tells you where to find notes. In tablature:

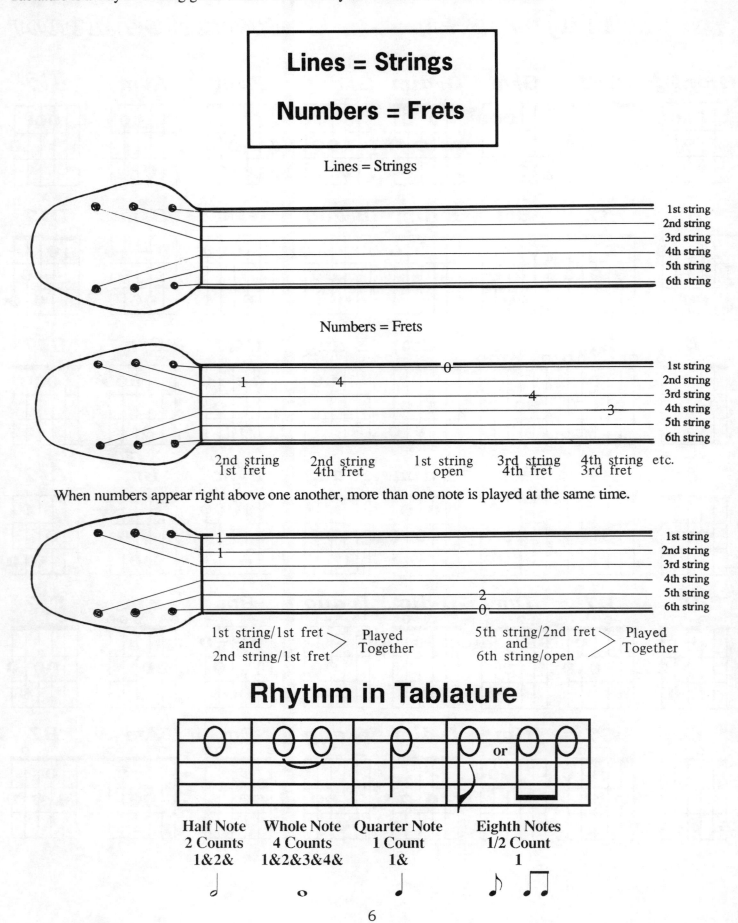

Lines = Strings

Numbers = Frets

Lines = Strings

1st string
2nd string
3rd string
4th string
5th string
6th string

Numbers = Frets

1st string
2nd string
3rd string
4th string
5th string
6th string

2nd string   2nd string   1st string   3rd string   4th string etc.
1st fret   4th fret   open   4th fret   3rd fret

When numbers appear right above one another, more than one note is played at the same time.

1st string
2nd string
3rd string
4th string
5th string
6th string

1st string/1st fret
and   Played
2nd string/1st fret   Together

5th string/2nd fret
and   Played
6th string/open   Together

Rhythm in Tablature

Half Note	Whole Note	Quarter Note	Eighth Notes
2 Counts	4 Counts	1 Count	1/2 Count
1&2&	1&2&3&4&	1&	1

ARPEGGIO PICKING (BROKEN CHORDS)

Arpeggio-style playing is especially beautiful when used as an accompaniment to a ballad. Basically all the player does is play the chord, a note at a time, starting from the bass note and moving up. The thumb (p) should rest on the bass note of the chord, and first finger (i) on the third string, the middle finger (m) on the second string, and the ring finger (a) on the first string.

Check the diagram to make certain your right-hand fingers are plucking the correct strings.

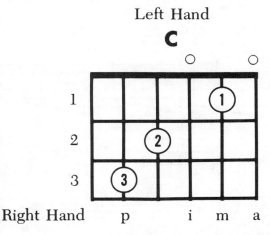

Hold a C Chord and Play: p - i - m - a

Arpeggio exercise:

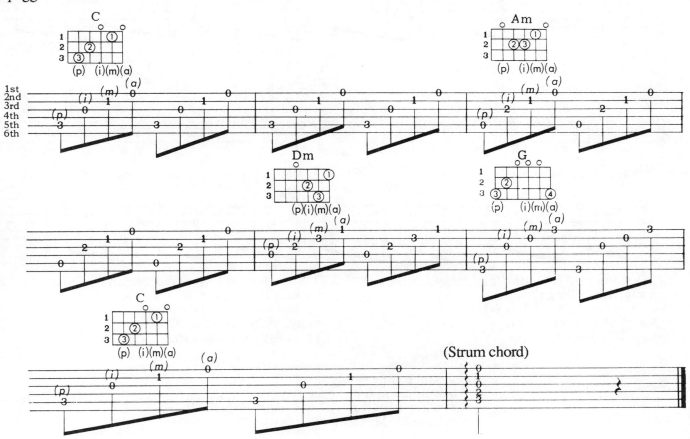

7

Shenandoah

2. The white man loved the Indian maiden,
   Away, you rolling river
   With notions his canoe was laden,
   Away, we're bound away,
   'Cross the wide Missouri.

3. O, Shenandoah, I love your daughter,
   Away, you rolling river
   I'll take her 'cross the rolling water,
   Away, we're bound away,
   'Cross the wide Missouri.

4. O, Shenandoah, I'm bound to leave you,
   Away, you rolling river,
   O, Shenandoah, I'll not deceive you,
   Away, we're bound away,
   'Cross the wide Missouri.

An interesting variation on the standard arpeggio picking is the use of alternate basses. With alternate basses, the guitarist plays the arpeggio as usual; however, an alternate bass note is plucked with the thumb the second time that the arpeggio is played.

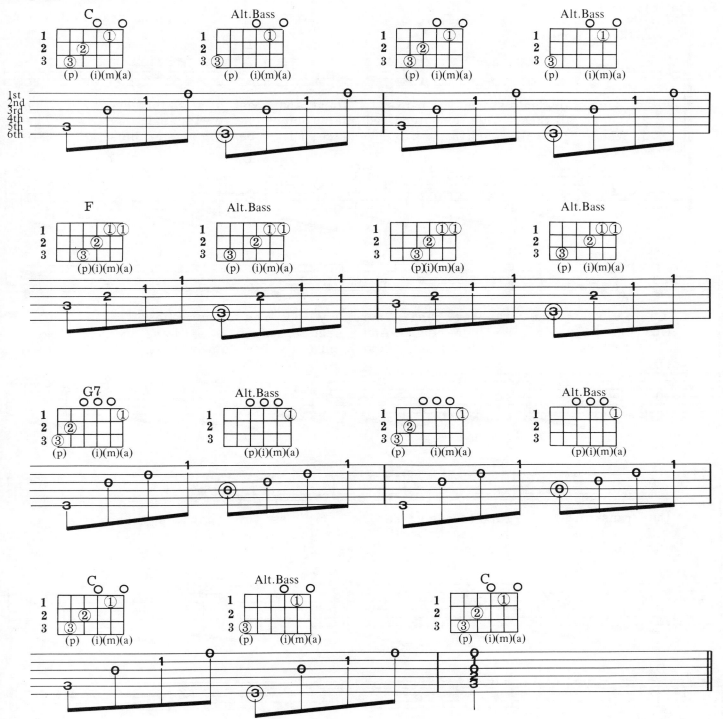

Alternate G7 Chord

This form of the G7 chord lends itself exceptionally well to fingerstyle playing. Try substituting it into songs in place of the standard G7 fingering.

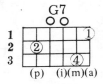

9

On Jordan's Stormy Banks

Samuel Stennett
1727-1795

American Folk Melody

1. On Jor-dan's storm-y banks I stand, And cast a wish-ful eye   To
2. O'er all those wide ex-tend-ed plains Shines one e-ter-nal day;   There
3. When I shall reach that hap-py place, I'll be for-ev-er blest,   For

Ca-naan's fair and hap-py land, Where my pos-ses-sions lie,   O___
God the Son for-ev-er-reigns, And scat-ters night a-way.   No___
I shall see my Fa-ther's face, And in his bos-om rest.   Filled

the trans-port-ing rap-turous scene That ris-es to my sight: Sweet
chill-ing winds of poi-sonous breath Can reach that health-ful shore;   Sick-
with de-light my rap-tured soul Lives out its earth-ly day;   And

fields ar-rayed in liv-ing green And riv-ers of de-light!
ness and sor-row, pain and death, Are felt and feared no more.
then, though Jor-dan's waves may roll, I'll fear-less launch a-way.

You will remember that in 3/4 time you count 1-2-3, 1-2-3, etc. The arpeggio pattern in 3/4 time is most commonly p-i-m-a-m-a. You simply play the standard arpeggio (p-i-m-a) and repeat the last two notes (m-a).

Exercise 1

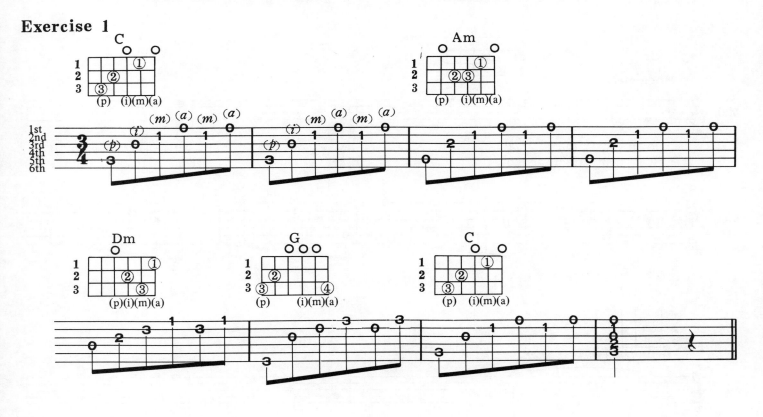

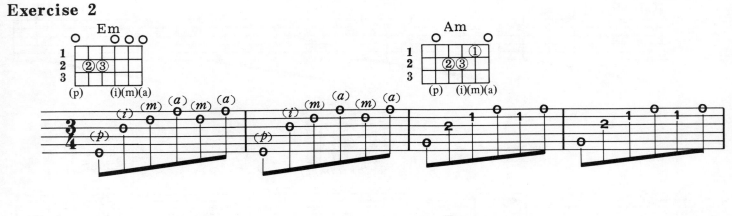

Exercise 2

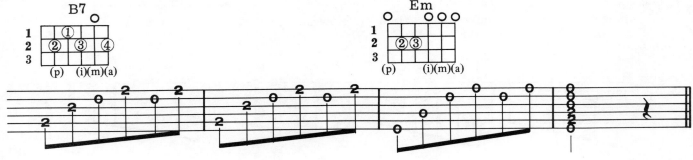

Down in the Valley

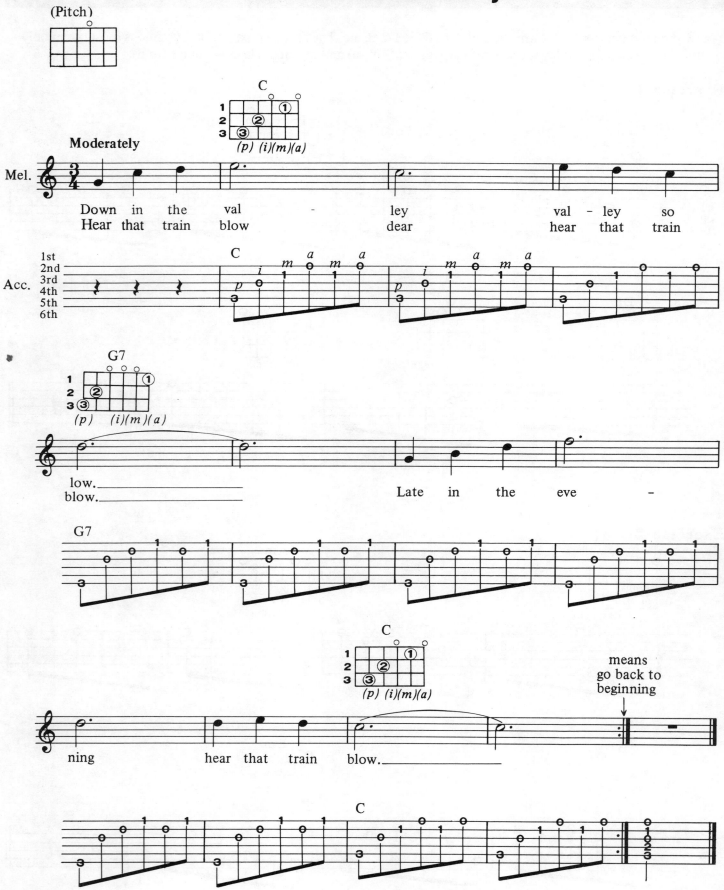

Try playing the following song, "Amazing Grace," with this finger pattern: p-i-m-a-m-i. This arpeggio pattern merely has the effect of going up and coming down. It is particularly suitable for slow ballads and hymns.

Amazing Grace

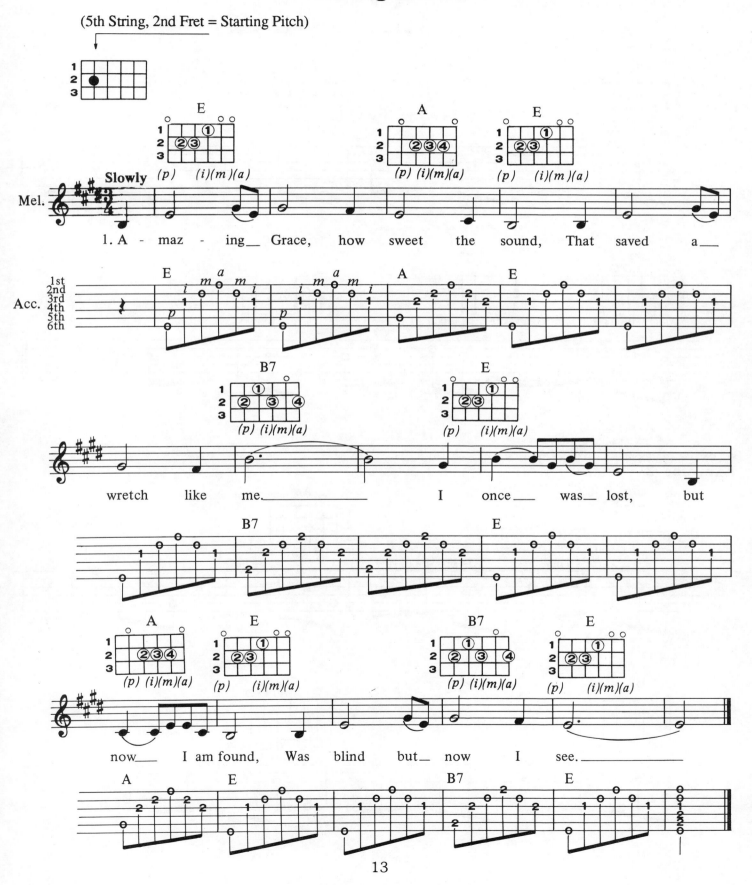

A triplet is counted: 1 - 2 - 3,   2 - 2 - 3,   3 - 2 - 3, etc.
                    one - trip - let,   two - trip - let,   three - trip - let

The pattern for the triplet arpeggio is: p - i - m   a - m - i

Exercise 1

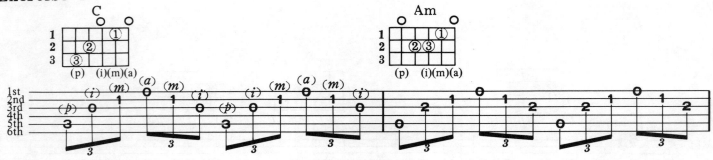

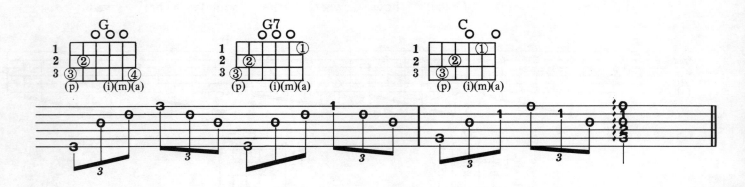

Exercise 2

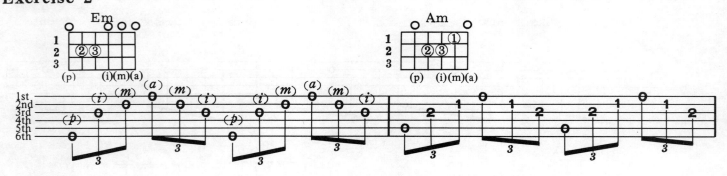

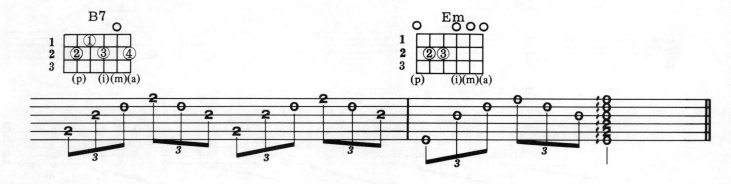

14

Aura Lee

P-i-m-i-a-i-m-i

Example 1

Example 2

Look Down

Spiritual

Look down,   look down_____   that
Look up,   look up,_____   and

lone   –   some   your road,_____   Be – fore   you
greet   your Mak – er   'Fore   Ga – briel

tra   –   vel   on._____
blows   his   horn._____

16

With this fingerstyle effect the guitarist first plucks the bass note with the thumb. This is followed by the index finger, the middle and ring fingers together, and back to the index finger. The important thing to remember is that the middle and ring fingers pluck together. Two notes should sound at once.

Bury Me Not on the Lone Prairie

Western Song

"Oh bu - ry me not _____ on the lone prai -
In a nar - row grave _____ just six by

rie!" _____ Where coy - otes howl _____
three _____ Oh bury me not _____

_____ and the wind blows free.
_____ on the lone prai - rie."

17

Hammering-on is an effect used widely in country and bluegrass picking. The player first plucks the bass note with the thumb, and then plucks the first, middle, and ring fingers simultaneously. Following this, the guitarist raises the middle left-hand finger off its string, plucks the string, and while this tone is ringing presses down the middle finger of the left hand. Finally, the first, middle, and ring fingers pluck their notes again simultaneously. This interesting pattern is not as complicated as it sounds. Remember that the effect is brought about largely by plucking an open string and then pressing down the left-hand middle finger while the open string is still ringing.

Hammering-On C Chord

Hammering-On F Chord

Hammering-On G Chord

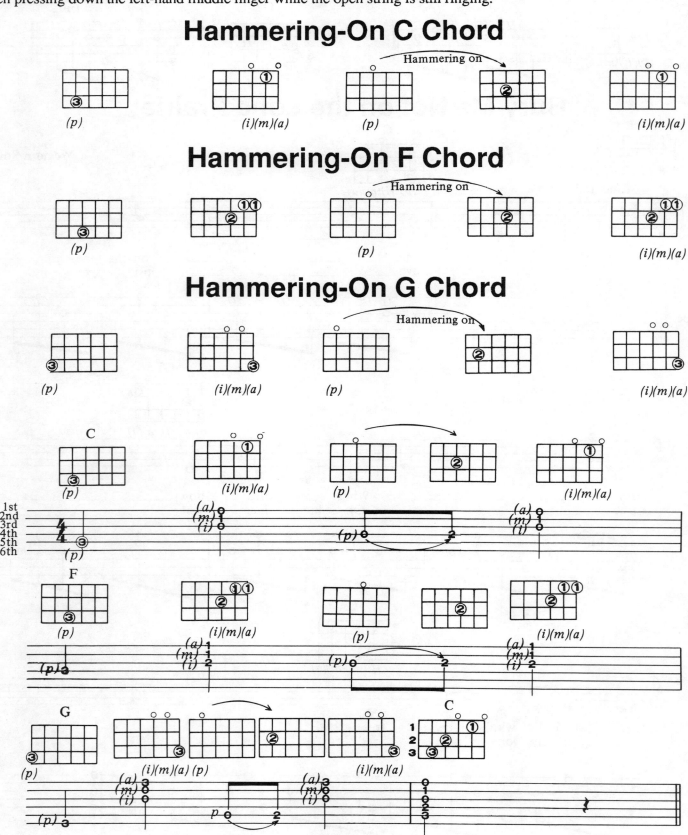

18

Careless Love
(Hammering-On Style)

Bluegrass Song

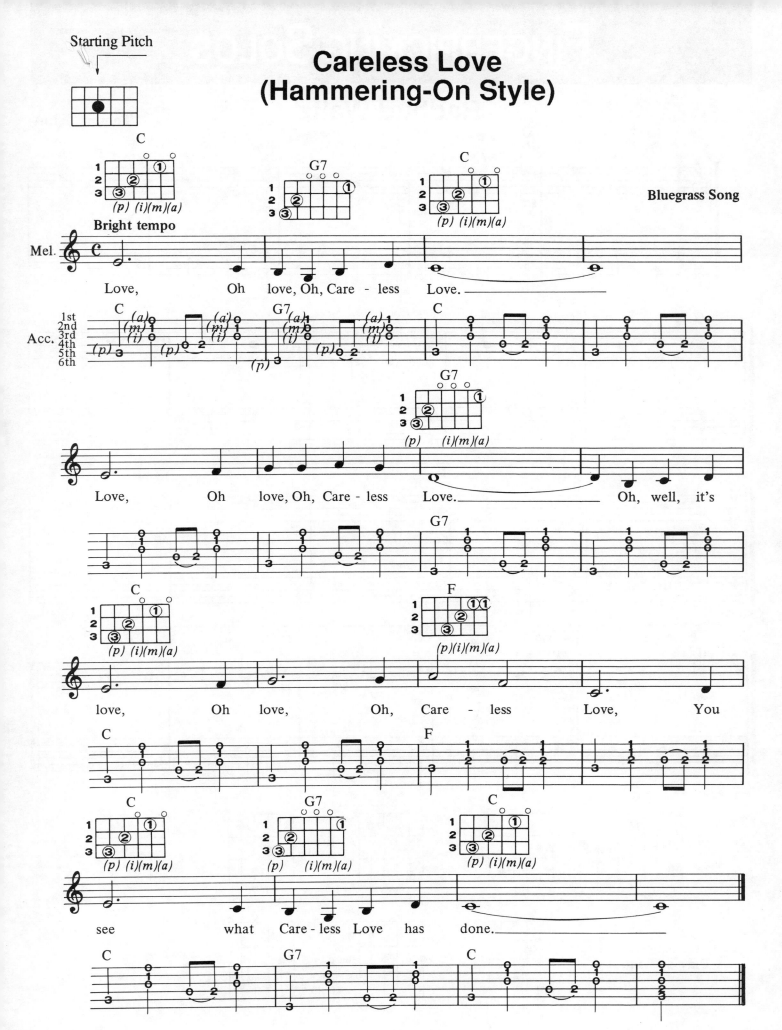

Redbud Waltz

Tommy Flint

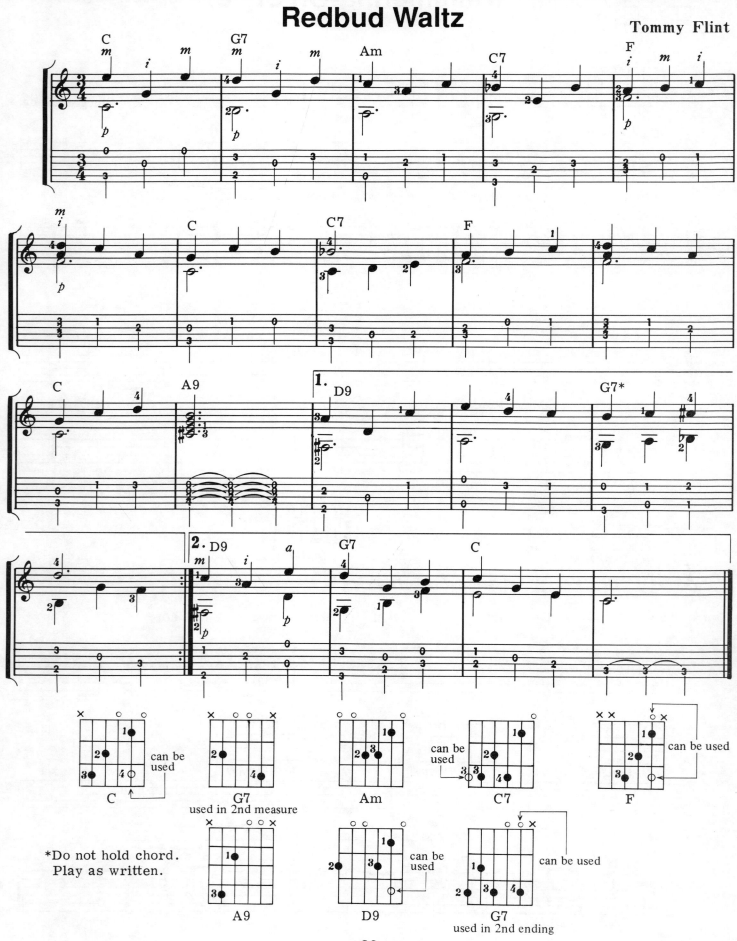

*Do not hold chord.
Play as written.

Early Spring

Tommy Flint

Huron Cove

Tommy Flint

Green Grow the Lilacs

Arr. Tommy Flint

* Do not hold chord. Play single notes.

The Hills of Brown

Tommy Flint

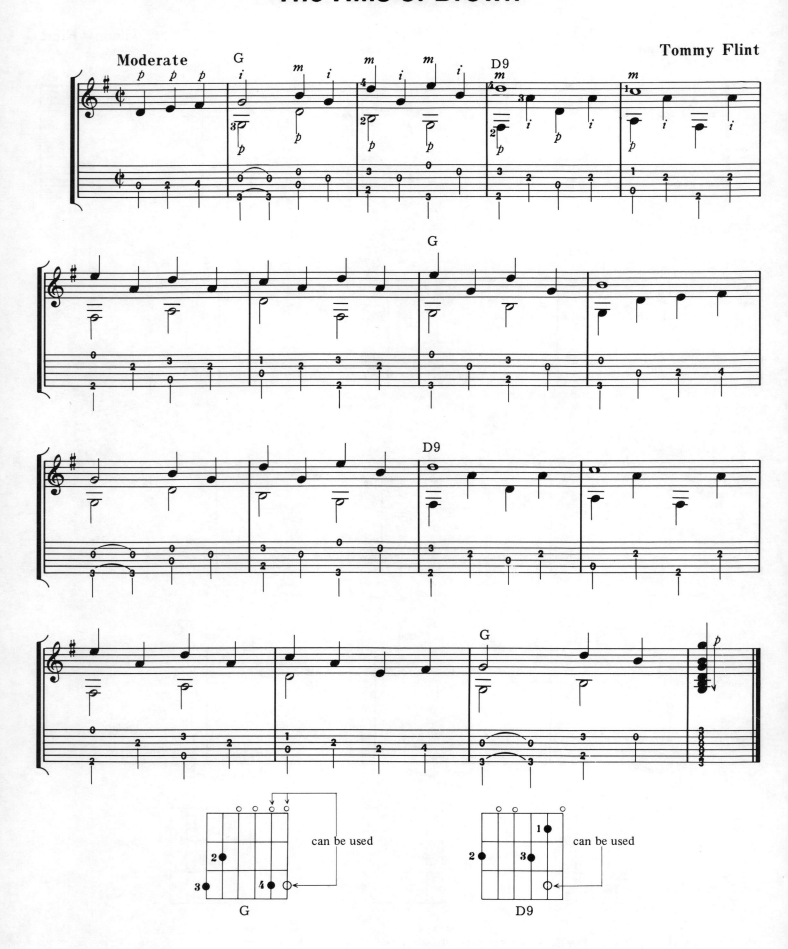